FRIENDS
OF ACPL

PLANTATION DOLL

BY
THE SAME AUTHOR:

SKELETON CAVE

PLANTATION DOLL

By
CORA CHENEY

Illustrated by
JO POLSENO

NEW YORK
HENRY HOLT AND COMPANY

Copyright, 1955, by Cora Cheney
All rights reserved, including the right to reproduce
this book or portions thereof in any form

In Canada, George J. McLeod, Ltd.

Library of Congress Catalog Card Number: 55-5889
91385-0215
Printed in the United States of America

CO. SCHOOLS

C478611

FOR
IRENE AND
HER SEVEN GIRL COUSINS
WHO ALL LOVE DOLLS
AND ATTICS
AND MYSTERIES

CONTENTS

CONTENTS

PLANTATION
DOLL

CHAPTER ONE

ROSE HILL

Aren't they ever coming, Mother?" asked Lucinda for the fifth time in thirty minutes.

"Don't be so impatient, Lucinda," replied Mrs. Jefferson as she snipped pink roses into her garden basket. "You know airplanes are often late."

"Mother, may I look at the red and blue rose?" asked Lucinda.

"Yes, but don't touch it. It looks like it's going to be just right for the flower show next week."

Lucinda and her mother leaned over to examine the bud that was forming on the stocky old bush.

"It's lovely," exclaimed Lucinda.

The outside of the bud was so dark it was almost blue, so the Jefferson family always called it the red and blue rose.

"Isn't it wonderful that it'll be in bloom in time for the flower show and while Molly and Aunt Marge are here?"

"Yes," said her mother. "It doesn't often bloom this early. It's been years since I've had one of these in time for the Flower and Antique Show. I've pinched off all the buds but this one so it will bloom faster. We must be very careful with it."

"Want me to carry the basket for you?" Lucinda asked.

"No, thanks. Why don't you go play with the boys in the sand pile?"

Lucinda looked down at her clean white

slippers and smoothed out her pink skirt. Her yellow curls lay softly on her shoulders. She made a pretty picture there in front of the old white house.

"I think I'll just sit in the swing. I don't want to get my clothes dirty. But I'd like to help you."

Mrs. Jefferson gave her daughter an inquiring look. Never had Lucinda been so helpful as she had been in the past few days. She had set the table for Dillie. She had dusted the dark furniture in the living room. She had tidied the table in the library, and she had helped polish the silver.

She had entertained her little brothers without being reminded. Mrs. Jefferson had an uneasy feeling that something was going on. Lucinda was just *too* good.

Lucinda gave a push with her foot and thought with pleasure of her cousin Molly and Aunt Marge who should be here any minute. They were coming all the way from New York to visit at Rose Hill Plantation.

"Mother, did Daddy and Aunt Marge sit in this very swing when they were children here at Rose Hill?"

"I suppose so," answered her mother.

"And I bet Aunt Marge played right here with Mamselle," Lucinda said.

The story of the disappearance of Mamselle was the mystery of Rose Hill. Mamselle

was a beautiful old French doll who had disappeared under strange circumstances when
Aunt Marge was a little girl. Nobody ever
knew what happened to her, and no trace of
her was ever found.

A little trunk of doll clothes still re-

mained, a family treasure, to remind them of the mysterious disappearance.

"I hope Aunt Marge has lots more stories to tell about Daddy, when he was a little boy," said Lucinda.

Mrs. Jefferson laughed. "I hope she won't tell too many tales about Daddy's mischief when he was little. The boys think up enough themselves without any new suggestions."

Mrs. Jefferson took her basket of blossoms and went into the house. Lucinda looked longingly down the road, straining her eyes for a sight of the familiar blue car that would bring Daddy and the company from the airport in the city. She couldn't wait to share her surprise with Molly.

She walked to the edge of the road, then back to the swing. She simply couldn't sit still.

Her little brothers were arguing over a

metal spade in the sand pile. Three-year-old Jimbo wasn't a match for five-year-old Danny. He let go the spade and angrily kicked over Danny's sand castle. Both children howled.

"You'd better quit. I'll tell Mother," threatened Lucinda.

She took her eyes from the road for a moment and didn't see the blue car approaching until it turned into the Rose Hill driveway.

CHAPTER TWO

THE COMPANY

Mother, they're here!"
shouted Lucinda.

Mrs. Jefferson came running to the door,
followed by Dillie, the cook. The little boys
came running too, forgetting their quarrel in
the excitement of the arrival of the company.

Aunt Marge, looking very citified in her
dark traveling suit, was waving out of the
car window. From the back seat a tall girl
with dark pigtails and a wide sailor hat on the
back of her head grinned and shouted.

Suddenly Lucinda was stricken with shyness. It had been over a year since she had seen her cousin Molly. She was not prepared for the big girl who jumped out of the car and, tearing off her hat and white gloves, grabbed Lucinda around the waist.

With huggings and kissings and "how-they've-grown's," the party moved up the steps to the house. Molly pulled her bag from the car and insisted on carrying it herself.

"I have my own suitcase this time," she announced proudly. "And I'm going to carry it myself, if you'll take these things," she continued as she handed Lucinda her hat and gloves. "Mother made me wear them. I don't like gloves."

"I think they're pretty," said Lucinda, examining the fashionable string gloves. "Gracious, Molly, you're so tall, and your hair is so long."

She felt one of the fat braids that hung over Molly's shoulders and admired the red-checked ribbons on the ends.

"Oh, Molly," continued Lucinda breathlessly as the girls entered the house. "Mother is going to let us sleep together in the polka-dot room."

"Really?" Molly set her bag down and turned to look at her cousin with wide, excited eyes. "Oh, Lucinda, aren't we going to have fun? Isn't it wonderful to be almost nine years old?"

She hugged her cousin again, and the two little girls ran up the curving stairs to the high-ceilinged room that was papered in rich blue with fat white dots all over it.

Molly laid her suitcase on the old four-

poster bed with its ruffled canopy and began to unfasten the clasps.

"Now what do you think I brought you?" she teased.

CHAPTER THREE

THE PRESENT

Is it something to eat?"
asked Lucinda.

"No, not to eat," replied Molly. She sat
down on the side of the bed beside the half-
open suitcase. This was fun. Lucinda would
never guess what it was.

"Do I wear it?" Lucinda inquired, star-
ing at the opening in the bag as if it could tell
her the answer.

"Nope," giggled Molly. "Well, maybe
you wear part of it."

Lucinda thought and thought. She pulled at one of her curls.

"Is it soft?" she begged.

"No. Well, part of it's soft."

"Molly Nelson, there just isn't any such thing. I bet you didn't bring me anything," Lucinda declared.

"I'll give you a hint," offered Molly. "It has lots of parts, and you play with it."

"You didn't bring me a set of wooden blocks, did you?" Lucinda asked cautiously.

Molly laughed. "Of course not. That's baby stuff."

"Well," sighed Lucinda. "I didn't know whether you remembered how big I am. Is it a book? If it isn't a book or a doll, why, I give up."

"It isn't a doll or a book, I'll tell you that much. But if you just *can't* guess, I'll give you another hint. It's playing like being some-thing that—well, it's playing like being someone that you see every day from September to June."

"September to June? But we go to school then. Oh, Molly, you've *got* to show me."

Molly opened the suitcase and drew out a large, square package wrapped in candy-striped red and white paper. She held it teasingly before her cousin.

"May I open it?" begged Lucinda, reaching for it.

Molly watched with a big grin while Lucinda tore off the paper. Inside was a box with LET'S PLAY SCHOOL written across the top. There was a picture of a classroom with a little girl playing teacher.

Inside the box was everything a school teacher would need. Together the girls laughed and exclaimed as they picked out the contents. There was a little blackboard and an eraser with white and colored chalk to go with it.

"This stick is for pointing," said Lucinda.

"Or for spanking the bad ones," added Molly.

Both girls giggled as Lucinda put a pair of tiny glasses on the end of her nose. "I am Miss Jefferson," she announced sternly.

"And I'll give you a bad grade," said Molly, drawing out a small set of report cards.

There was a roll book, a pencil which wrote red on one end and blue on the other, and a pair of scissors. There was a bottle of ink and a pen, and paste, and colored paper.

"Look, there's even a little ruler," exclaimed Lucinda.

"And look here. There are sheets with numbers and letters written on them," added Molly.

"I learned my numbers and letters a long time ago," remarked Lucinda.

"Me too," said Molly.

"Oh, Molly, this is the most wonderful

present. Thank you so much for it. We'll have a real school when we play with it. And now, I've got a surprise for you."

"For me?" asked Molly.

"But you'll never guess. Come on—Uncle Rab can't wait to show it to you."

CHAPTER FOUR

UNCLE RAB

Uncle Rab was an old Negro who lived in a log cabin below the vegetable garden at Rose Hill. He had lived there since before Molly's and Lucinda's parents were born.

He was too old to work much, but he puttered in the garden and helped out where he could. On good days he sat on his little porch in the sun with his cat who had recently produced a family of frisky kittens.

Dillie was his daughter. Three times a

day Uncle Rab walked up to the big house for his meals, or Lucinda, Mrs. Jefferson, or Dillie took him his food. Dillie washed his clothes and cleaned up his house, but his real pleasure in life was the children.

Jimbo and Danny visited him daily, and Lucinda took great care of the old man, advising him to be careful of drafts and to be sure and keep his feet dry. In return, Uncle Rab spent his time making small gifts and telling them tall stories.

"Molly's coming to see us," Lucinda had breathlessly announced one day as she ran in to see the old man. "We've got to do something special for her."

Uncle Rab sat in the warm, southern sun and smiled to himself.

"I said Molly's coming," repeated Lucinda a little sharply.

"I was just thinking about a goat," replied Uncle Rab.

"A goat?" Lucinda shook her head sadly. Uncle Rab was really getting too old to be sensible. "What's that got to do with Molly?"

"Miss Marge had a goat," Uncle Rab continued dreamily, "and that little Molly's just like her mama."

"Aunt Marge had a goat?" Lucinda asked. "I never heard about it. When did she have a goat?"

"When she was about your size. Her papa got it for her when she was grieving about losing her doll baby."

"You mean after she lost Mamselle?" asked Lucinda.

"That child grieved for that dolly until her papa said he'd do anything to make her happy. And what did she want but a goat. Well, he got her one." Uncle Rab closed his eyes and sat quietly.

"What happened to the goat?" prodded Lucinda.

"That goat was so bad that your grandma said her grief was soon going to be worse than Miss Marge's. Your poor grandpa was torn both ways." Uncle Rab stopped again.

"Then what happened?" Lucinda reminded impatiently.

"Old goat got in the roses, and he had to be sent away to a farmer who raised goats. Since then there's mostly just been kittens at Rose Hill." Uncle Rab paused to stroke the ears of the mother cat who was purring by his ankles.

"But I think goats are nice for little children," Uncle Rab sighed. "And I know where there's a little goat looking for a nice home. I'd take him if I thought some little girls would look after him and feed him. I might even make a little harness for him."

CHAPTER FIVE

A CONSPIRACY

Lucinda stood right up in front of Uncle Rab.

"Uncle Rab Jefferson, you know you're teasing me. Don't tease me, Uncle Rab! Oh, how I'd love to have a little goat cart when Molly comes. But I know Mother would never let me. She has so much to do, keeping the big house clean and the flowers growing, with only Dillie to help." Lucinda ended her long speech on a sad sigh.

"Maybe if you'd help your mama more, she'd let you have a goat."

"I do help her, lots. I look after Jimbo and Danny," answered Lucinda. "Maybe if you'd help more with the garden she'd let us have a goat. Anyhow, I don't believe you even know a goat that needs a home."

Maybe this was only one of Uncle Rab's stories.

"Yes, I do," chuckled Uncle Rab. "Boy over at Magnolia told me at church that he had a nice little goat that wanted a home. I could take him and let him live right here behind my house, but your mama might not like it. And what'll we feed him?"

Lucinda sat silently thinking about right and wrong. Finally she made a decision.

"Tell you what, Uncle Rab. If you'll get that goat and make a little harness, I'll bring you the little wagon I used to play with. I'll bring the goat his food from the kitchen. Then after Molly comes we'll ride him around to the front of the house, like it was a surprise present for Molly. I don't think they'll make us undo what's done."

Uncle Rab considered the ethics of this plan and found it satisfactory.

"I'll get the goat," he promised, "but you've got to keep Jimbo and Danny away from here, honey, if you don't want the others to know."

So Lucinda had outdone herself keeping the boys busy and away from Uncle Rab's house.

Uncle Rab took some scraps of leather and made a small harness for the goat. And Lucinda quietly brought the little wagon down to his house.

The day before the company was to arrive, Uncle Rab made a rare excursion from home and came back after dark leading the little goat.

"Oh, Uncle Rab, he's perfect!" Lucinda cried when she saw the goat early the next morning. "We'll let Molly name him," she decided.

What more could she ask of life except that the day hurry by? And wouldn't Molly be tickled *pink*? And wouldn't the grownups be surprised when she and Molly came riding around to the front of the house in the goat cart?

And now the moment was here! She and Molly ran hand in hand down the slope to Uncle Rab's house where the goat was waiting.

CHAPTER SIX

SURPRISE!

Uncle Rab was sitting on his porch, waiting for the children. He patted Molly's hand and called her "little Marge."

"Just like your mama," he said.

Lucinda was impatient. "The surprise, Uncle Rab. Let's show Molly."

"Is it the kittens?" Molly wanted to know, seeing the tiny balls of fur playing by the hearth in Uncle Rab's house.

"Better than kittens," Lucinda told her.

Uncle Rab rose and led the way to the rear of his cabin. The goat was already harnessed and hitched to the little wagon.

"Ohhhhhh," squealed Molly. She ran over and patted the goat who was pawing with annoyance at being tied and harnessed.

Lucinda excitedly explained about the goat and how none of the grownups knew the secret. While Uncle Rab smiled and Lucinda talked, Molly ran around and around the goat. She examined the tiny harness and the clever way that Uncle Rab had attached the wagon.

"And we're going to let you name him, Molly," concluded Lucinda.

Molly put her finger on her chin and frowned thoughtfully. "What about, what about," she paused, "what about Surprise? Why don't we name him Surprise?"

"Of course," cried Lucinda, "that's a wonderful name. He surprised you, and he's going to surprise the grownups, too."

Surprise was not a very large goat, and Lucinda's wagon was not very large either.

"Reckon he can pull us both, Uncle Rab?" asked Lucinda.

Uncle Rab looked at the healthy pair of little girls and scratched his head.

"Let's try him one at a time," he suggested. "Then when you get to the corner of the big house you can both squeeze in and ride around to the front steps together."

"You go first, Molly," said Lucinda generously, although she was longing to take the first ride.

"Thanks," replied Molly.

She sat down in the little wagon and tucked her feet under herself. Uncle Rab untied Surprise, and Molly shook out the little reins.

The girls squealed with delight as the procession started off. Uncle Rab walked in front, half-leading, half-pulling the surprised Surprise.

At the corner of the garden Molly insisted on stopping to let Lucinda ride. Surprise gave a long "baaaa" when he was prodded into starting again.

Luckily Dillie didn't see them as they walked through the back yard. The rest of the household was comfortably settled on the porch, having cool drinks.

Molly and Lucinda put their hands over their mouths to quiet their giggles as they approached the corner of the house. Then Molly climbed in behind Lucinda, and Uncle Rab stepped behind, leaving the girls to drive in state to the front steps.

CHAPTER SEVEN

AN UPSET

Jimbo saw them first and let out a yell that startled Surprise. Molly and Lucinda, seeing the astonished faces of the grownups, let their giggles go free.

"What on earth?" shouted Mr. Jefferson.

"Lucinda!" exclaimed her mother.

"Molly Nelson, where did you get that goat?" cried Aunt Marge.

"It's a goat and cart, it's a goat and cart," shrieked Danny over and over.

Dillie came running from the kitchen.

"Lord have mercy," she cried, "where did they get that goat?"

C478611
CO. SCHOOLS

The little boys crowded around while the girls shouted with excited laughter. It was too much for Surprise. The combination of noise, people, and the unfamiliar harness, frightened him. He began to tremble and twitch and gave a mighty leap forward, upsetting the wagon.

Lucinda and Molly were thrown into a squealing heap on the ground. The wagon overturned and dragged upside down behind the disappearing goat.

As Surprise turned the corner, the clattering wagon caught in one of the pink rose-bushes. The goat yanked and pulled, tearing the bush. Then the harness broke, leaving the battered wagon behind. Surprise fled in the direction of Uncle Rab's house, bleating as he ran.

Molly and Lucinda found themselves

being picked up and dusted off by their
mothers. Mr. Jefferson was holding the boys,
who were planning to chase Surprise.

Dillie saw Uncle Rab standing quietly in
the background.

"Pappy," she said accusingly, "you ought to be ashamed of yourself."

Mr. Jefferson looked serious. Aunt Marge, reassured that Molly and Lucinda were unhurt, greeted Uncle Rab, who was glad to avoid Dillie's baleful eyes.

Lucinda explained to her father and mother about how she and Uncle Rab wanted to surprise everyone, especially Molly and Aunt Marge.

"Well, you certainly did surprise us," agreed her father.

"I'll fix up this rosebush right now, Mr. Jefferson," Uncle Rab began, feeling a little responsible for the unexpected performance of the goat. "Good thing it wasn't that rosebush Mrs. Jefferson is guarding for the flower show."

"It surely is a good thing," whispered Molly to Lucinda, "or we might not get to keep Surprise."

"May we keep him, Daddy?" begged Lucinda.

"He looks like the goat I used to have," Aunt Marge remarked. "Remember how sad we were when Papa sent him away?"

"I do remember, and I bet you do too, Uncle Rab," laughed Mr. Jefferson. "Now, girls, will you take care of him? Feed him? Keep him out of mischief?"

"Oh, yes, sir," the girls promised eagerly.

Mr. Jefferson examined the broken harness.

"We'll get Uncle Rab to fix up the harness, and we can let the goat have the old toolshed for his house. But you mustn't scare him. Only one child at a time in the wagon, and don't make him tired. If you prove that you can take proper care of him, we'll see about letting him stay."

Molly and Lucinda sat down on the steps with glasses of lemonade, and the little boys ran off with Uncle Rab to help install Surprise in his new home.

CHAPTER EIGHT

BEFORE SUPPER

Mrs. Jefferson went in the house to help Dillie get supper ready while Mr. Jefferson and Uncle Rab tied up the damaged rosebush.

Aunt Marge, who had slipped into a cool, cotton dress, brought a cushion and sat down beside the girls on the steps.

"Isn't the red and blue rosebud lovely?" said Aunt Marge. "It's bound to win the prize in the Flower and Antique Show. Why, I remember that rosebush when I was a litttle girl and how people used to come here just to see such an odd flower."

"We're glad Surprise didn't hurt *that* bush," said Lucinda.

"Goats seem to have a way of getting into the rosebushes here at Rose Hill," Aunt Marge admitted ruefully.

"Let's hope Surprise won't be like your goat," said Lucinda. "I wish you'd tell Molly and me about him," she said hopefully.

Aunt Marge searched her memory and drew out the story of her goat who had been sent away after getting into the rosebushes.

"And now," she said as she finished the tale, "you girls certainly need to wash your faces. And change your clothes," she added, looking at Molly's new travel dress which had been soiled in the upset.

"If we hurry, Mother, will you tell us another story before supper—about old days here at Rose Hill?" begged Molly.

"Maybe," replied her mother.

Molly and Lucinda clattered up the stairs. Molly's mother had unpacked her daughter's suitcase. Her summer dresses were hanging neatly in the closet beside Lucinda's, which had been moved into the polka-dot room for the occasion.

Lucinda usually slept in the little bedroom next to her parents' room downstairs, but since she and Molly were getting so big they were being allowed to sleep in one of the two guest rooms on the second floor.

"Let's dress alike," said Lucinda. "Do you have a yellow dress?"

"Yes," replied Molly, "but it's my party dress. I'd rather wear jeans."

The girls washed their faces and hands and combed their hair in front of the shadowy, old mirror.

"Mother said I had to wear dresses in the evening at Rose Hill. I have a red dress," Molly said.

"So do I," cried Lucinda.

Molly produced her dress.

"It's a lot like mine," said Lucinda, taking hers from a hanger, "except mine has checks."

Looking like a pair of little ladies, they were soon back with Aunt Marge, who called them her twins and put an affectionate arm around each of them.

"Now, what kind of story?" Aunt Marge asked.

"The story of Mamselle," Molly suggested promptly.

"Aren't you tired of hearing about Mamselle?" teased Aunt Marge.

"Oh, no," replied both girls.

Jimbo and Danny appeared around the corner.

"Stories!" shouted Danny. Both boys ran and settled themselves at Aunt Marge's feet, ready to listen.

CHAPTER NINE

MAMSELLE

O nce upon a time," began Aunt Marge, "about ninety years ago, when your great-grandmother was a little girl, someone gave her a beautiful doll."

"Who gave it to her?" interrupted Danny.

"Her godmother brought it from France," replied Aunt Marge, "and your great-grandmother named the doll Mamselle, after the French word *mademoiselle* which means 'miss.'

"She was about twelve inches high, and

she had a kid body and a bisque-china head. She had deep blue eyes that opened and shut, and she had eyelashes that curled up in a black fringe around her eyes."

Aunt Marge paused, remembering. The children were absorbed and big-eyed.

"Oh, my, she was beautiful," she continued. "She had real hair that was curled in long, black ringlets that could hang down her back or be tied in her tiny snood.

"Her feet and legs and arms and hands were made of china, and she even had little toenails and fingernails painted on to look like real ones."

"Don't forget what came with her," reminded Lucinda.

"Did anything come with her?" teased Aunt Marge.

"Of course, Mother, don't you remember the trunk?" said Molly earnestly.

"Oh, yes," Aunt Marge continued smilingly, "the trunk. Well, since she had come from so far away she had brought a trunk with her."

"I know that trunk," said Jimbo. "Mamselle's trunk is in the attic now."

"That's right," replied Aunt Marge. "The little leather trunk about the size of a big shoebox held Mamselle's clothes. You all know about the clothes, so I won't tell that part."

"Oh, please, please," the children all protested. "We want you to tell about the clothes anyhow."

"Very well," Aunt Marge agreed. "She had two pairs of tiny leather shoes with high heels. One was a pair of white kid pumps, and one was a pair of black, high-topped shoes that laced up. I believe they are the tiniest and daintiest shoes in the world. She had two pairs of stockings to go with them, made of soft, cotton. One pair was black, one was white."

"That's not all," prompted Lucinda.

"I haven't forgotten," answered Aunt Marge. "And the most amazing thing she had was a little corset just like old-fashioned ladies wore. It had little supporters that held up the stockings, and it laced up just like a real one."

Lucinda sighed dreamily. How she wished she could see the doll fine enough to wear such a wardrobe!

"Now tell about the dresses," said Molly.

"She had four dresses. Two for morning, one for afternoon, one for evening. One of the morning dresses was of dark red wool with a high neck. The other one was of blue checked cotton with a little white collar."

"That was the one she was wearing when she got lost," said Lucinda.

"Yes," replied Aunt Marge, "that's the dress you children have never seen."

"I'm glad she wasn't wearing her yellow

dress when she disappeared," said Molly.

"Yes, the afternoon dress is so pretty. It's pale yellow dimity with little roses pinned here and there on the ruffled skirt."

"That's the dress with the parasol to match, isn't it?" asked Danny.

"That's right," Aunt Marge replied. "There's a little yellow parasol to go with it, and a little yellow straw hat trimmed with roses."

"Don't forget the you-know-whats," prompted Lucinda.

"What could that be?" Aunt Marge looked questioningly around as if she had forgotten.

"The mitts!" cried both the girls.

"Oh, of course. She had some tiny white lace mitts, little gloves without any fingers."

"I wish I could have seen her with her mitts on," sighed Molly.

"But her evening gown of blue velvet was

the best of all," Aunt Marge went on. "It was cut very low in front, and it had a hoop skirt. It was trimmed with white lace that just barely showed around the bottom, and peeped out at the neck. She had a little white lace shawl to go over her head, and she wore a black velvet cape with a fur collar over the dress.

"There was a fur muff to match. I'm glad we still have the trunk of clothes, because they are the prettiest doll clothes I ever saw."

"You forgot the nightgowns," reminded Lucinda.

"Oh, yes, she had two white cotton gowns trimmed with lace and a little nightcap. And I almost forgot to mention that she had two pairs of white cotton drawers with lace on the legs. She had a white cotton petticoat and a red flannel petticoat and an embroidered linen one. Oh my, she was a lovely doll with a lovely outfit."

CHAPTER TEN

WHAT HAPPENED?

What happened to her?" asked Jimbo.

Aunt Marge began to look sad.

"One day when I was about Molly's and Lucinda's size I was allowed to play with Mamselle as a special treat. It was raining, and I was playing alone in the attic with her. I had my little puppy with me too, and I was pretending that he was a horse. I had taken a shoebox and colored it and cut it down so it would look like a carriage.

"I hitched the box up to the puppy and put Mamselle in it so she could go for a ride. Just as the ride started, your father called me from downstairs, and I went halfway down the attic stairs to answer.

"I was only gone a moment. When I came back, the puppy was romping about with the little box wagon still tied to him—but Mamselle wasn't in it."

"Ohhhhh," sighed Jimbo. "Poor Mamselle."

"I looked around a little bit," continued Aunt Marge, "because I thought she'd just fallen out; but I didn't see her anywhere. Her pretty clothes were lying in the trunk just as I had left them. She had been wearing her blue checked morning dress and a little hat I had made her out of some bird feathers. I was pretending that she was just riding around to see a sick friend, not going to a party."

"Poor dolly," exclaimed Danny.

"Mamselle wasn't anywhere. I looked all over the floor, and I looked in the trunk, and then I ran and looked down the stairs. I still couldn't find her.

"I began to get awfully frightened, and I looked everywhere again. Then I called my brother Dan.

"Dan came up and helped me look, but he couldn't find her either. I began to cry. Dan went downstairs and got our mother. She came up and began to look too. Our papa was at home, and he came and looked too, and Uncle Rab came up and looked.

"They all asked me over and over about what I was doing with her and where I was playing and lots of other questions. But Mamselle just wasn't there.

"My mama went through everything in the attic. We even looked in boxes and places she couldn't possibly be, but we never did find her. Nobody knows to this day what happened to her.

"I still think about it and feel like she must be in the attic somewhere. She couldn't have gotten out. All the windows were shut, and there was nobody else there to take her away."

"Maybe the puppy ate her," suggested Danny.

Aunt Marge laughed and stood up.

"I don't think so, Danny. After all, she was a very substantial doll, made to last."

Just then Mrs. Jefferson stepped out on the porch to call them in to supper, and the children followed their mothers into the house.

"Oh, Lucinda," breathed Molly, "wouldn't it be wonderful if we could find her? Let's try looking very hard for her."

CHAPTER ELEVEN

THE ATTIC

When Molly and Lucinda woke up in the polka-dot room the next morning, they lay under the sheet and whispered for a while. Molly looked up at the ruffled canopy above the bed and told Lucinda that it looked like a giant hat to her.

Lucinda said it made her feel like she was in a little house. And that reminded her of her little house in the attic.

The attic had two big dormer windows in the front, and in the alcove lived Lucinda's doll family. There she kept her doll furniture and dolls, her tea set, and her doll clothes.

"You haven't seen the dolls yet," whispered Lucinda.

Molly jumped up eagerly.

"I want to go see them right now," she announced. "Shall we wear jeans?"

"No, let's wear dresses if we're going to play dolls," said Lucinda.

The girls dressed themselves quickly in their red dresses they had worn the evening before, and ran barefooted up the attic stairs.

"Oh, Lucinda, you've got a new doll!" exclaimed Molly, picking up a lovely girl doll with dark, curly hair.

"That's Susie," said Lucinda. "I got her for Christmas. She looks a little like I think Mamselle looked, but not so pretty of course."

"I guess no doll was ever as pretty as Mamselle," said Molly. "You know, while we're up here I'm going to look for her."

"It's no use," said Lucinda. "Everybody's been looking for her for years and years. She just vanished."

"Well, she couldn't just vanish," said Molly. "I still think I'm going to look."

Molly walked to the middle of the attic. Starting at the ceiling, she looked up and down the walls and rafters, turning slowly so her eyes missed nothing.

Lucinda was sitting cross-legged on the floor, dressing Susie. She watched Molly a moment, then stood up to join her.

"Maybe two pairs of eyes looking at the same time might find her. Maybe two people never stood here and looked together," said Lucinda.

"Let's try it," said Molly.

"Shall we make up a spell?" asked Lucinda.

"Wonderful! You make up one," said Molly.

Lucinda thought a moment.

"How's this? Let's hold hands and shut our eyes and turn around three times and say a verse. Then wherever we stop, it means that's the direction to look in."

"Have you got a verse?" asked Molly.

"No, but we can each make up one."

Both girls stood and thought a moment.

"How's this?" giggled Molly. "Mamselle, Mamselle, if I see you I will yell."

Lucinda giggled too. "I like that. Here's mine. Dolly with a lovely face, come out from your hiding place."

"Fine," said Molly. "Yours is really pretty."

The girls joined hands and shut their eyes and turned slowly, saying the verses in low tones. When they stopped they were facing the window in the doll alcove.

"Oh, Molly," said Lucinda, "I don't think spells do any good. She can't possibly be in that direction."

"No, I don't see how she could be. There's just no place to look there. Maybe it means she fell out the window, but I don't believe that either. I think Mamselle's in this attic still."

"Sometimes I think so too, but I don't think there's any sense in looking again. It's been done so many times."

"Well, I'm going to look a little more anyhow," said Molly. She pulled out a few boxes and peered under some old furniture and searched on some shelves.

"I guess you're right," she admitted finally. "I wish we could play with Mamselle's clothes."

"I know where they are," said Lucinda. "Mother won't mind, if we're careful."

The girls undid the tiny trunk and examined the clothes.

"They don't fit any of my dolls," said Lucinda. "Besides, I don't think they ought to be put on any other doll anyhow."

"Neither do I," said Molly. Together they folded the clothes back into the little trunk. "But maybe someday something will happen to lead us to Mamselle."

"Maybe," agreed Lucinda. "Do you remember this doll?"

"Oh, sure, that's Coobaby. And isn't that
May behind you? I wish she could be my doll
while I'm here."

"Of course she can," said Lucinda. "I'll
get you some clothes for her. You know
Mother used to dress up kittens when she was
a little girl. I wish Uncle Rab would let us
play with some of his kittens."

"We can ask him," said Molly. "If he'd
lend us the kittens we could dress them up and
have a doll tea party up here."

"I'm—" both girls began and then
stopped, laughing.

"Hungry!" completed Molly.

"I think I hear Dillie ringing the breakfast bell now," said Lucinda.

With May and Susie under their arms, the
girls ran down the stairs to breakfast.

CHAPTER TWELVE

LITTLE BOTHERS

Lucinda and Molly smoothed the covers on the canopied bed and hung up their nightclothes.

"I guess we'd better put on our shoes," suggested Lucinda. "Mother doesn't like us to go out of the house barefooted. And we'll want to see Surprise this morning."

The girls discovered that they had twin pairs of red sneakers which they could only tell apart because Molly's were a half size longer.

"Why don't we take May and Susie with

us and then we can take them to ride in the goat cart?" said Molly.

Uncle Rab was waiting for them on the back steps with Jimbo and Danny on either side of him.

"Lucinda, Mother says you all have to watch us this morning," announced Danny.

"Keep us from trouble," added Jimbo.

Lucinda gave a long, injured sigh.

"I wish," she remarked to Molly, "that we might have some time for our own affairs."

"Little children must play nice," Uncle Rab reminded them.

"Play nice," echoed Jimbo.

"But we want to ride in the goat cart," announced Lucinda.

"Little brothers got rights too," said Uncle Rab.

"Little *bothers*," muttered Lucinda.

Molly giggled. "Couldn't we all ride in the goat cart?" she asked.

"Oh, please, Uncle Rab," begged the children.

Uncle Rab rubbed his chin and agreed to harness up Surprise to the wagon.

"Littlest go first," decreed Uncle Rab, helping Jimbo into the wagon. He held the rein that guided the goat and led the crowing Jimbo around the garden.

"Me next," cried Danny. Danny had picked up a long, slender stick which he planned to use for a switch.

"I'm going to go *fast*," he announced.

"No, you're not," replied Lucinda firmly. "Uncle Rab, tell him he can't ride this like a Roman chariot."

Uncle Rab took the switch, and Danny had a tame ride around the yard.

Molly chose to go last, but she walked along beside Lucinda, who sat primly in the cart with Susie clutched in her arms. Lucinda in turn walked beside Molly while she and

May had a ride.

"Little goat's tired now," said Uncle Rab. "Let's tie him back of my house to rest."

"I'm going to ride some more," bragged Danny.

"No, you're not," the others told him.

"I will so," said Danny. "I'm almost six years old, and I'm big enough. You'll see. I'll ride him all by myself someday, as fast as I want to."

CHAPTER THIRTEEN

THE BACK-YARD SCHOOL

Uncle Rab tied Surprise securely to the tree behind his house, and the children stood by watching the little goat eat. Dillie had saved table scraps for him. Jimbo pulled up some sweet grass and poked it in front of Surprise's nose.

Surprise grabbed the grass greedily, licking Jimbo's fingers. Jimbo squealed, and the other children shouted with laughter.

"Let's do something else," suggested Lucinda after Surprise had eaten all he could hold.

"What about the tea party?" Molly asked in a low voice.

"It won't be any fun if we have to watch the boys. They'll wreck everything," Lucinda whispered. "We'd better do something that's fun and can amuse them at the same time."

"Why don't we play school?" Molly suggested.

"Oh, the very thing! We can have school on the back steps, and if the boys aren't good Mother will be near to make them behave."

"What's that about the boys?" asked Danny, curious at the muffled conversation.

"We're going to have school," said Lucinda, "out on the back steps."

"I don't want to go to school," replied Danny.

"Yes, you do," urged Molly. "We're going to play school with the school teacher set I brought to Lucinda. We're going to share with you boys."

"Well," replied Danny, "maybe I'll come."

"I want to play school if Uncle Rab will come too," Jimbo said.

"Uncle Rab's too old to go to school, honey," replied the old man.

"Oh, come on, Uncle Rab," begged the children.

Uncle Rab finally consented. While Lucinda ran upstairs to get her school teacher set, the other children settled themselves on the back steps.

"We'll have to have a desk for me," Lucinda decided when she returned to find her four pupils all ready to start classes. "All right, Uncle Rab, you're the biggest. You'll have to get me a desk."

Uncle Rab gazed around the yard until his eyes fell on two saw horses. These he moved over by Lucinda and placed a plank across the top.

"Now I need a seat," said Lucinda.

Uncle Rab located a keg in the woodshed and placed it behind the makeshift desk.

"Thank you." Lucinda smiled at Uncle Rab, who once more seated himself on the steps.

The children gathered around as Lucinda opened the box and laid her supplies out on the desk.

"What's that?" asked Jimbo, picking up the roll book.

"Don't you know anything? That's the— that's the—uh . . ." said Danny.

"I don't think you know much about it, Mr. Smarty," said Lucinda. "You've never been to school. That's a roll book."

"Well, I'm going to school this fall," answered Danny, "and I can already write my name and do lots of things."

"Then you'll have a chance to show us,"

said Lucinda primly as she laid paper, cray-
ons, pencils, paste, and scissors in orderly
piles.

"I like this pencil," said Jimbo, seizing
the red and blue teacher's pencil.

"That's for the teacher," said Lucinda as
she placed her glasses on the end of her nose
and took the pencil in her hand.

Molly and Danny began to giggle.

"Silence," demanded Lucinda, who was
writing names in the roll book. She took the
small blackboard in her hand and looked for
a place to hang it.

"Why not hang it on the side of the
woodshed, sugar," said Uncle Rab.

Lucinda looked through her glasses at
Uncle Rab and frowned.

"You don't call your teacher 'sugar,'" she
replied sternly.

Uncle Rab looked down at his feet, hanging his head in mock disgrace. Lucinda

propped the blackboard up on the desk with a pair of bricks.

Danny and Molly were whispering behind their hands, and Jimbo began yawning and squirming.

"The class will come to order," Lucinda began, making a sharp rap with her pencil.

"To order?" cried Jimbo. "Are we going to order something?"

Danny and Molly broke out in squeals of laughter. Jimbo, shamed by his mistake, began to ball his face up for a cry. Uncle Rab, trying hard not to smile, reached over to lift Jimbo onto his lap.

"Quiet!" shouted Lucinda to the giggling older ones. "No lap-sitting," she ordered the old man and the little boy.

Jimbo snuggled up close to Uncle Rab and gave a drowsy little sigh.

"Now I'll call the roll," began the teacher. "Molly Nelson."

"Present."

"Daniel Franklin Jefferson, III."

"Present."

"Uncle Rab Jefferson."

"Right here."

"No, Uncle Rab, say 'present,' " insisted Lucinda.

"All right, honey, I'm present."

"Don't call me 'honey'! I'm Miss Jefferson."

"All right, Miss Jefferson. Present."

"James Boaz Jefferson."

"I don't have any present." The puzzled Jimbo sadly held out his empty hands.

Lucinda rapped for silence again as Molly and Danny once more squealed with laughter.

"Now we'll have spelling," began the teacher. "Molly Nelson, how do you spell 'flag'?"

"F-a-l-g," answered Molly.

"Wrong. Daniel Jefferson, how do you spell 'flag'?"

"Me? I can't spell," answered Danny. "All I can do is write my name."

"Uncle Rab?"

"I don't believe I rightly remember," Uncle Rab began, scratching the back of his head.

"Jimbo's gone to sleep," remarked Molly.

"Don't change the subject," the teacher replied primly. "F-l-a-g spells 'flag,' " she told them, writing on the small blackboard with red chalk.

"F-l-a-g," repeated the children dutifully after her.

"Now we will salute the flag," the teacher remembered. Things weren't running quite in order. But maybe nobody would realize that spelling lessons weren't supposed to come before flag salute.

"But there isn't any flag to salute," suggested Danny.

Molly volunteered to go get the small flag out of the library, and when she returned they had a very impressive Pledge of Allegiance.

"Now we'll have arithmetic," said the teacher. "Molly, what is nine take away three?"

"Six," replied Molly quickly.

"Uncle Rab, add one to thirteen."

There was no answer.

"Uncle Rab," said the teacher sharply, "add one to thirteen."

But Uncle Rab, sitting in the warm sun, had followed Jimbo in a little snooze. He came to with a start.

"Who got one tooth hurtin'?" he asked, half-awake.

"*Uncle Rab!*" cried Lucinda, joining the others in their laughter.

"Why not let May and Susie be in the school?" Molly asked when the children had quieted down. She pointed to the two dolls who were propped up under the tree. "I can answer for May, and Danny can answer for Susie."

"Very well, let's enroll the new pupils," the teacher agreed, writing their names in the roll book. "Molly and Danny may be excused to get the new pupils."

Molly picked up May and was bringing her carefully back to the steps when she noticed that Danny was carrying Susie upside down by one leg and was holding his nose with his free hand. Danny motioned to Jimbo, who was awake now, to see the horrible trick he was playing on the teacher and his sister's doll.

"Look what he's doing!" shrieked Molly, reaching out to grab Susie from her dangerous situation. Danny was caught off balance and stumbled over a rock. He fell with Susie under him.

Molly yelled, Lucinda howled, and with

both girls landing on top of him Danny began to bellow.

Uncle Rab separated the scrapping children just as Mrs. Jefferson appeared at the back door with a tray and a long, sharp knife in her hand. The children looked up, startled.

"Isn't it about time for recess?" she asked. "Uncle Rab, would you please go get the watermelon out of the tub of water in the basement. I think it's about time we cut a watermelon for the kinfolks."

The children flopped down on the steps.

"My!" said Danny. "It really scared me when I saw Mother standing there with that big knife. I thought we'd had one fight too many and that she was *really* coming after us."

CHAPTER FOURTEEN

WATERMELON TIME

Uncle Rab brought the
big melon from the basement and laid it on
the tray Mrs. Jefferson had ready. Aunt
Marge stood by, holding salt and forks.

Mr. Jefferson, who was at home that day,
came out of the house to cut the luscious
melon into juicy wedges. The children ate
their pieces and ran to Uncle Rab with the
rinds.

"Would you make us some watermelon
teeth, please?" they begged.

Uncle Rab took his pocket knife and made thin slivers of the white rind just the size to fit inside the children's lips. On these he carved little ridges to resemble huge teeth. He cut a tiny hole in the middle and ran a piece of the red melon through it to make a tongue.

Molly's was finished first. When she slipped the false teeth inside her mouth the children shouted with laughter.

Soon all the children had watermelon teeth in their mouths and ran to show the grown folks. Danny laughed so hard that his teeth fell out on the ground. He picked up the dirty set and decided to go back to the pile of rinds and make some more.

Nobody was looking. Danny picked up one of the wet rinds and slipped up behind Lucinda.

"Your face needs washing," he shouted, wiping the rind all over his sister's face.

Lucinda gave a blood-chilling yell that

made her false teeth shoot like a rocket out of her mouth. Mr. Jefferson reached out a long arm to catch Danny.

Lucinda, her face dripping with water-melon juice, picked up the discarded rind and hurled it blindly in the direction of her

brother. Unfortunately it missed its target and hit Mr. Jefferson squarely in the head.

"Enough!" shouted Mrs. Jefferson, who was barely able to control her laughter at the sight of her husband's wild expression.

Aunt Marge, convulsed with laughter, dropped to the porch steps while Uncle Rab ran for a bucket of water to wash the messy hands and faces.

Mr. Jefferson wiped his face and gave a

strained laugh.

"Lucinda," he remarked, "from now on let *me* take care of punishments. And as for you, Danny, if you ever pull a stunt like that again I'll give you the worst face-washing you ever had."

"Yes, sir," replied both children meekly, "we won't forget."

CHAPTER FIFTEEN

THE DRESS-UP CLOSET

Underneath the attic stairs at Rose Hill was a closet with a tiny window to light it. There, in past times, the ladies of Rose Hill had hung cast-off dresses, hats, and shoes. Old school costumes had been added. To the children at Rose Hill it was known as the Dress-up Closet. There were makings for all sorts of outfits.

"Let's dress up," Lucinda suggested the next morning.

Molly and Lucinda opened the small

door and began to pull out funny old clothes. Jimbo and Danny soon joined them, although the girls were not too enthusiastic about having them.

"Why not dress the boys for your children?" suggested Mrs. Jefferson, who was coming down the attic stairs.

"Oh, Lucinda, let's!" said Molly.

This was fun. Molly dressed Jimbo like a little girl. She put an old straw bonnet on his head and tied it with a big pink ribbon under his chin. She found a pair of high button shoes, several sizes too large for his fat little feet. An old shirtwaist with a wide, blue satin sash made a dress that came to his ankles.

Jimbo was delighted with himself. He found a pair of gloves that hung limply on his small hands.

"I'm an old-timey girl, I'm an old-timey girl," he cried as he ran about, flapping his hands together.

Danny, who was not holding very still, was making less progress at becoming an old-fashioned boy. Lucinda had found a pair of red-striped stockings and a small pair of boy slippers with red pompons on them. To this she added a pair of baggy wool knickers.

Molly laughed until she had to sit down when Lucinda put an oversized shirt on the little boy and tied a big bow under his chin. She perched a little sailor hat on the top of his head.

Meantime the girls were inspecting and rejecting garments for themselves.

Molly finally chose a lovely, blue satin, embroidered kimono that had been brought from Japan many years before. Lucinda helped her make it shorter by tucking the waist up under a sash.

"I'll pin up my pigtails and put flowers behind my ears," remarked Molly as she helped Lucinda button herself into an old-fashioned white dress. Her pantalets showed out from below the skirt. Lucinda pulled her yellow curls forward and put a battered little bonnet on her head.

"You both need parasols," said Danny.

"Of course," agreed Lucinda. "I have a paper Japanese one in my room that you can use, Molly."

Danny went down to his sister's room for the parasol. And Molly helped Lucinda drape white tulle over her mother's regular umbrella.

"This will make it look like Mamselle's lace one," Lucinda said.

Molly pinned her black braids into two little mounds on the sides of her head. Then the four children paraded to the back yard where Molly picked two big zinnias to stick behind her ears.

"Now, let's play like we're visitors," Lucinda suggested, "and walk around and come up the path to the front door."

Their mothers were sitting on the steps, shelling butter beans for dinner. They were talking about the Flower and Antique Show.

"Oh, my goodness," cried Mrs. Jefferson as the children approached. "Company's coming, and here we are in our old house dresses, shelling butter beans."

"We're trapped," groaned Aunt Marge. "And they're strangers at that."

The visitors tried very hard not to laugh. It almost seemed that their mothers really didn't recognize them.

"Won't you sit down," said Mrs. Jefferson cordially.

The strangers settled themselves on the steps with a few snickers.

"You must be the new family who's moved in under the attic stairs," said Aunt Marge politely. "Is this your little girl?" she asked, pointing to Jimbo.

"No, it's me," said Jimbo in distress.

"Gracious, you look like a strange little girl to me," said Mrs. Jefferson, peering at him.

"No, no, Mother. See, it's me. I'm Jimbo," he cried, tearing off the bonnet and gloves.

"Oh, of course," said Mrs. Jefferson, taking him into her lap. "You certainly fooled me that time."

"I'm still not sure about these ladies," said Aunt Marge, "or this young man."

"Anyhow, I think they need some lemonade," said Mrs. Jefferson. "You entertain them, Marge, while I run make some."

"Yum," cried Danny, pulling off his costume. "I'm always ready for lemonade."

CHAPTER SIXTEEN

THE TEA PARTY

When the girls were putting the clothes back in the Dress-up Closet, Molly suggested the doll tea party again.

"Wouldn't it be neat to dress up in lady clothes and have it down under the hedge?" she added.

"Oh, my yes," Lucinda replied. "And I'd like to do it without the boys."

"Me, too," agreed Molly.

Happily they made their plans for the

next day when they were to bring their dolls down to the high hedge below the garden. There the old shrubs had not been clipped in a long time. Two opposite rows met overhead, making a delightfully private little house underneath.

Life at Rose Hill was busy. Mr. Jefferson was away at his law office in town during the daytime. Mrs. Jefferson was occupied with entertaining Aunt Marge and making and receiving calls from old friends. Dillie had her hands full with extra cooking.

"You girls will have to watch the little boys again today," Mrs. Jefferson announced at breakfast. "Aunt Marge and I are going to have lunch with Cousin Annie Sue and attend to some business about the flower show. Dillie is going to change the beds. I'll have to count on you all to keep the boys out of mischief."

"Yes, m'am, Mother," Lucinda agreed half-heartedly. How could they ever manage to carry out their plans if they had to watch the boys?

Mrs. Jefferson and Aunt Marge got ready to go out, first stopping to inspect the red and blue rose.

"It's perfect," said Mrs. Jefferson. "It's bound to win a ribbon. We can pick it early tomorrow morning, and it will be opened just enough to show the red center."

Lucinda and Molly rather unhappily watched their mothers depart. They sat on the steps, keeping watchful eyes on the two boys in the sandpile and considering the day before them. The costumes for the tea party hung enticingly in the Dress-up Closet.

"I was going to be a young lady and wear those green high-heeled slippers," said Lucinda disconsolately.

"I was thinking of being a grandmother and wearing those high button shoes and putting my hair in a big knot," said Molly. "And I was going to wear that old middy blouse and the long, black skirt."

"I don't see why we can't tell the boys to go see Uncle Rab," mused Lucinda. "Then maybe we could have a quick tea party."

"Tell you what," said Molly. "Why couldn't you go get the cookies out of the kitchen while I get a pitcher of water? Then we can carry the dolls and your tea set down to the hedge, sort of taking turns watching the boys."

"Wonderful!" replied Lucinda. "When we get everything all ready we can tell the boys to go see Uncle Rab. Then we can dress and have our party in a hurry."

"Then when the party's over we'll be close to Uncle Rab's house and we can go get them. I don't think they can get in trouble if we have just a short party," Molly added.

The girls busied themselves making their

preparations while the boys played nicely in the sand pile. They took turns carrying the dolls and the food down to the hedge. Dillie was busy with her cleaning, and Uncle Rab was nowhere in sight.

Finally everything was ready, and the costumes were laid out for a quick change.

"Why don't you all go down and see Uncle Rab for a while," Lucinda suggested to the boys.

"May we?" asked Danny in surprise.

"Oh, sure," Lucinda replied. "Molly and I will come down to get you after a while. You visit Uncle Rab until we come."

Danny and Jimbo ran off in the direction of Uncle Rab's house. The girls went quietly upstairs and put on the lady clothes. Dillie was singing at her work and didn't hear the girls stumbling down the back stairs.

It was a delightful tea party. Lucinda was the mother. She sat on a chair made of a pile of leaves with her feet stretched out before her, showing off her high-heeled green shoes.

The dolls, her children, were arranged around the little hedge house. The tea set was laid out neatly on a box table.

Molly was the grandmother coming to visit. She knocked on the door.

"Come in," said Lucinda cordially, stumbling slightly as she rose to her feet. The green shoes tended to bend inward, and as she tried to support her weight on the table, the tea set was spilled to the ground.

Grandmother Molly came on in and helped pick up the dishes.

"What a lovely house!" she exclaimed. "And what beautiful children!"

Lucinda replied that sometimes her children gave her a little trouble. Some of them didn't want to go to sleep at night. Others were bad about getting in the cookies. Some of them scrapped and argued. The ladies agreed that raising a family had its problems.

"Won't you have some tea?" Lucinda asked.

"I'd be delighted," replied Molly.

As they drank their water tea and ate their

cookies, they discussed the problems of keeping house under a hedge and swapped recipes
for cookies. They were having a beautiful
time and quite forgot the little boys until they
heard a terrible shriek from the front yard.

CHAPTER SEVENTEEN

DISASTER

Meanwhile Danny and Jimbo had gone down to Uncle Rab's house. The old man was nowhere in sight. Everything was quiet.

"Uncle Rab," called Danny, sticking his head in the open door. "Uncle Rab's not home," he told Jimbo. "I guess we better just wait here a few minutes to see if he comes back."

"Let's look at Surprise," Jimbo suggested.

In a minute the boys were poking around

in back of Uncle Rab's house. Surprise was tied to the small fence behind the house, contentedly eating grass.

"Oh, Jimbo," whispered Danny. "Why don't we hitch him up and ride fast like I wanted to. I said I was going to, and now's my chance."

Jimbo's eyes began to sparkle.

"Let's just walk Surprise around to the front of the house and hitch him up there. I think the wagon's in the woodhouse. Then I'll ride him down the driveway *real* fast." Danny hurriedly untied the goat while he talked.

"Now we'll tie him to the hitching post," Danny continued when they reached the front steps, "and we can go get the wagon."

Jimbo helped Danny tie up the goat to the old, iron hitching post with a long rope. Surprise nibbled a little grass, and the boys ran to get the wagon and harness.

But the wagon wasn't in the woodhouse, and it took several minutes to locate it out by the little goat's shed. Then they had to go back to the woodhouse to look for the harness. When they returned to the front of the

house, Dillie was just coming out the front door.

At that instant Dillie screamed. The frightened boys looked first at Dillie, then beyond her. Surprise, still tied by his long

rope, had wandered into the red and blue rosebush!

"Get that goat! Get that goat!" yelled Dillie. "He's eating the red and blue rose!"

"Uncle Rab! Lucinda!" screamed Danny. "Come help us!"

"Oh, he ate Mother's roooooose," wailed Jimbo.

CHAPTER EIGHTEEN

THE KITTEN

Lucinda and Molly heard the racket and were jerked back from their make-believe world. They exchanged a horrified look, then without a word tore off the hobbling skirts and shoes and ran like scared rabbits to the front yard.

They arrived just as Uncle Rab appeared from the opposite direction. Danny had just dragged the goat from the midst of the red and blue rosebush.

The prize blossom was gone, eaten by the little goat.

Jimbo and Danny stood silently, dropping their heads in guilt. Lucinda began to cry. Molly looked from one to the other, trying to piece together what had happened.

Dillie, softened by the sight of the tears,

checked the angry storm of words that came to her lips.

"I thought you girls were looking after the little boys," she said.

"We were supposed to be," sobbed Lucinda. "Oh, Mother will be so disappointed." Her voice rose to a pathetic wail.

"Who let the goat out?" Uncle Rab asked sternly.

"I did," admitted Danny in a low voice.

Jimbo joined Lucinda in a loud burst of sobs.

"We didn't mean to let him eat the red and blue rose." Two tears ran down Danny's nose and dropped to his hands. "The girls said we could go to Uncle Rab's. When he wasn't home, we decided to hitch up Surprise and ride him fast like I wanted to."

Jimbo's wails rose higher.

"Oh, stop crying, you children, and tell what happened," Dillie demanded.

"We went back to get the wagon," said Danny, "after we brought Surprise up. We did tie him to the hitching post, but I guess the rope was too long. I didn't even think about his eating the roses."

"Your mama's going to be awful mad," Dillie said. "Lucky the bush isn't hurt, but there won't be any prize rose from Rose Hill this year."

The four children sat sorrowfully on the steps.

"It was my fault," said Lucinda. "I was responsible for the boys."

"No, it was mine," replied Molly. "I suggested the tea party."

"I let Surprise out," said Danny.

"I was a bad boy," whispered Jimbo. And he climbed into Lucinda's lap and cried a few more tears on her shoulder.

Lucinda and Molly quietly took off the rest of their dress-up clothes and returned the dolls and dishes to the doll alcove in the attic. Dillie served their lunch in cold silence, and nobody was hungry at all.

Jimbo was put to bed for a nap, and the three older children sat in a sad little group on the back steps.

"There'll be more roses next year. The bush isn't hurt," comforted Uncle Rab.

"But the prize blossom! Mother was so proud of it," mourned Lucinda.

"Maybe somebody'll cheer up if they have a kitten to play with," suggested the old man.

"Really, Uncle Rab?" Lucinda looked up with a spark of interest. Uncle Rab never allowed them to play with his kittens.

"Uncle Rab," asked Molly cautiously, "would you let us take one of the kittens to the attic so we could play dolls with it?"

Uncle Rab thought it over for a minute.

"I reckon so, honey, but you mustn't play

too hard with my kitten. Have to be gentle. Danny, you run down to my house and bring the black one. He's the biggest."

Danny returned in a moment with the tiny black kitten in his arms. Molly was allowed to carry it to the attic, and Lucinda was allowed to choose the doll clothes in which they planned to dress it.

The children were so happy with the new plaything that they almost forgot the sorrow-

ful news that they must tell their mothers. Lucinda picked out a white blouse and a pink skirt for the kitten. Molly found a little straw hat, and two pairs of doll shoes which they put on the four paws.

The kitten scampered and clawed at its feet, clowned with its tail, and rolled over in play.

The girls looked for dresses for their dolls while Danny played with the kitten.

"It makes me think of the time Mother lost Mamselle," said Molly. "Except she had a puppy," she added.

"Do you think we could hitch a cart to the kitten," suggested Danny, "like Aunt Marge did to the puppy?"

"I think there's been enough doings about a cart today," said Lucinda firmly.

Danny agreed. "I think I'll go get my teddy bear," he said. "I'll be back in a minute."

CHAPTER NINETEEN

LOST

Lucinda and Molly picked up their dolls while the kitten scampered about between them, biting at the doll shoes on its feet.

"If we can find two more white blouses and some skirts, we can dress May and Susie like the kitten. Then we can put them all in the doll carriage and maybe take them for a ride down to Uncle Rab's house," chattered Lucinda.

Molly finished dressing May just as Danny reappeared with his teddy bear.

"Where's the kitten?" he asked.

"Why, it's right here," said Lucinda, looking about her. "Where *is* the kitten?" she added in a puzzled voice.

Molly looked up with a startled expression. "Oh, it must be hiding."

"Kitty, kitty," called the children.

Molly and Lucinda laid down their dolls and began running about the attic, looking under boxes and among the toys. Danny ran and looked down the attic stairs.

The three children exchanged a look of panic. Had they all gone crazy? The kitten had been with them just a minute ago, and now she was gone.

Molly and Lucinda ran and looked down the stairs too, but it would have been impossible for the kitten to have escaped that way. Frantically the three looked again in every corner and under and behind every box and trunk in the attic.

"She couldn't fall out the windows," cried Lucinda in desperation. "The screens are locked in tight."

"Let's sit down and think," Molly suggested.

The children stopped and covered their eyes with their hands, thinking. In the silence they heard a faint mew and a scratching sound.

"What's that?" asked Lucinda in a loud whisper.

"It's the kitten," whispered Molly.

"Where's it coming from?" asked Danny.

"Hush," said Molly.

Again it came, very faintly, the mewing, scratching sound.

"Where *is* the noise?" asked Lucinda. "It sounds like it's coming from downstairs."

Molly laid her ear to the floor.

"It does, almost," she admitted, "but how *could* it?"

The three children crawled slowly along the floor, stopping to listen when the faint sounds rose to their ears.

"It sounds like it's coming from under here," whispered Lucinda.

They huddled together and listened as

the unmistakable cries of the kitten came up through the floor.

"You all stay here," commanded Lucinda. "I'm going to run downstairs and see where the noise is coming from. We're just above the polka-dot room now, but I don't

see how the kitten could have gotten down there."

"Wait," cried Molly. "See the little hole under the floor board, where the rafter doesn't quite touch the wall? Over there," she pointed, laying her head on the floor to see better, "where the floor doesn't quite touch the wall, underneath the dormer?"

Lucinda and Danny put their faces to the floor to see the little opening that Molly's sharp eyes had caught.

"I believe it's big enough for a kitten to squeeze into," Molly breathed excitedly.

"Of course," cried Lucinda. "Oh, the poor kitten. She's caught in the *wall*, and with shoes on her feet she can't climb out!"

CHAPTER TWENTY

AND FOUND!

The children ran down to the polka-dot room and placed their heads against the wall here and there. There was no noise.

"Wait," cried Molly, opening the closet door. "Maybe this is the wall."

They crowded into the closet, and a faint mewing could be heard when they pressed their ears to the wall.

"I think we'd better call Uncle Rab. He'll have to cut a hole in the wall, or something," stated Lucinda.

"Oh, dear," moaned Molly. "Now Uncle Rab will be mad at us, too, for getting his kitten into trouble. It looks like this is our day to do wrong."

"But we'll have to call him, and quickly," replied Lucinda. "The kitten might smother if we don't get her out. Uncle Rab will know what to do."

"Uncle Rab! Dillie!" they called. "Come help us!"

Dillie was up the stairs in two seconds.

"You children," she threatened, "if you're in trouble again I'm going to tell your mamas to hire you a nurse."

Uncle Rab, who had been dozing on the back steps, was only a few feet behind Dillie.

"Uncle Rab," quavered Lucinda, "the kitten's in the wall! She fell down a little hole in the attic floor."

Uncle Rab brushed the children and Dillie aside and listened to the sound in the closet wall.

"Dillie, go fetch me the hatchet," demanded Uncle Rab.

"Pappy, you're not going to cut any hole in this wall," Dillie stated flatly. "I'm not going to face Mrs. Jefferson with the rosebush all ruined and now with a hole chopped in the wall."

Dillie stood defiantly, her arms folded as if nothing could move her.

"But, Dillie, we can't let the kitten *die* in the wall," cried Molly and Lucinda together. "Please go get the hatchet."

"If you don't go get the hatchet, Dillie," threatened Uncle Rab, "I'll take a pick from the tool shed and smash this wall."

Dillie reluctantly moved to get the hatchet. Danny ran back to the attic to try to see down the little hole.

Dillie was muttering and grumbling as she returned with the hatchet.

"Stand back, children," said Uncle Rab. "Let's don't get hit when I'm chopping."

He gave a strong whack at the plaster closet wall, then paused as the mewing sound was heard more clearly. From the attic came Danny's voice through the opening.

"Find her, Uncle Rab?" he called.

"Not yet, honey. Now one more whack," replied Uncle Rab.

The plaster fell in a dusty heap on the floor, and there was the sound of breaking wood as the thin laths broke under the hatchet blows. Behind was visible a small crevice between two supporting wooden posts.

The kitten could be plainly heard now, and the girls expected to see her fall to the floor.

"Something's in the way," remarked Uncle Rab. He dropped to his knees and ran his long arm up into the opening. "Something else is caught in the wall," he grunted, pulling

at a bulky object which was stuck in the nar-
row space.

Lucinda and Molly drew close, putting
their heads near the opening in the wall.

"What is it? What is it?" they asked.

"Why can't we get the kitten out?"

Uncle Rab gave a mighty jerk and fell backward. The obstacle pulled free, and the kitten scrambled unhurt to the bottom of the shute. Lucinda and Molly jumped aside just in time. Laughing with relief at the sight of the unharmed kitten, they reached out their hands to help Uncle Rab get up.

They saw it at the same time, the object in his hand.

"Uncle Rab!" they shouted. "It's a doll! It's a doll in your hand!"

Uncle Rab for the first time looked at the little bundle in his hand.

"Lord have mercy on my soul—if it isn't your great-grandma's lost doll!" he exclaimed.

CHAPTER TWENTY-ONE

PLANTATION DOLL

Let me hold her!"

"Let me see her!"

Uncle Rab, with maddening delibera-
tion, got up from the floor and disregarded
the girls. He brought the doll into the room
and laid her tenderly on the bed.

"Nobody's going to touch yet. She's so
old she might come to pieces," he declared.

Danny, Lucinda, and Molly crowded
about the tiny bundle on the bed while Uncle
Rab rescued the kitten they had all forgotten.

Dillie was cleaning up the mess on the closet floor.

Mamselle stared coolly at her rescuers. Although her hair was full of cobwebs and her face was dirty, her dress frayed and her shoestrings broken, she was still the poised, beautiful queen of dolls.

The girls stared at her in silence, hardly

daring to touch her. The dreamlike quality of actually having Mamselle here on the high bed in the polka-dot room made the children awkward and shy.

"I'll go get her clothes," offered Danny.

"Of course," said the girls as they came back to reality and gingerly stretched out their fingers to touch Mamselle. Lucinda found a soft hairbrush, and Molly got a damp washcloth. They didn't hear the car coming up the driveway.

"Where is everybody?" called Mrs. Jefferson's cheerful voice from the back door where she and Aunt Marge were setting down the bags of groceries they had brought from town.

The children jumped with surprise. Suddenly they remembered the terrible tragedy of the morning—the devastated rosebush.

"Mother, come quick!" cried Lucinda.

"We're in the polka-dot room," added Molly.

"We'd better tell them about the rose-bush first," whispered Lucinda.

The girls met their mothers at the bed-room door. Danny, who was just returning with Mamselle's clothes, joined them in the doorway. Jimbo, waking and hearing his mother, trotted up the steps.

"What's up?" asked Aunt Marge.

"Anything the matter?" asked Mrs. Jefferson with a questioning look. She saw Dillie and Uncle Rab in the room beyond. "Is anybody hurt? Are you all right?" she continued anxiously. The children were behaving so strangely.

"Mother," began Lucinda bravely, "there isn't going to be any prize blossom."

"We didn't watch the boys well enough," confessed Molly.

"And I let Surprise out," Danny admitted, hanging his head.

"I was a bad boy," whispered Jimbo.

"Ahhhhhh," sighed Mrs. Jefferson as her

eyes grew sad and her face took on a look of disappointment.

"Bush's not ruined, Mrs. Jefferson," Uncle Rab came forward to reassure. "But old Surprise really ate up the blossom. Rose Hill won't win any prize in the flower show this year."

"I think you girls ought to be very much ashamed," said Aunt Marge tartly.

"Suppose something had happened to the boys through your carelessness," added Mrs. Jefferson.

"We are ashamed," said Lucinda and Molly sadly.

"I'm ashamed too," said Danny.

"Shame," said Jimbo, hiding his head on his mother's skirt.

"But now, Mother and Aunt Marge," announced Lucinda, "we have something to show you on the bed. It's a surprise—especially for Aunt Marge."

"Shut your eyes," commanded Molly, "and we'll lead you in."

Each of the girls took their mother's hand and led them to the bed.

"Now," they cried, "look!"

"Mamselle!" cried Aunt Marge, picking up the exquisite old doll.

"How? Where?" asked Mrs. Jefferson, her eyes taking in the doll, the dustpan full of plaster, and the hole in the closet wall.

Everybody talked at once. Dillie gave her version. Uncle Rab gave his, Molly and Lucinda gave theirs, and Danny added his bit. While everybody talked and shouted and interrupted, Aunt Marge sat down and began undressing Mamselle.

"My frisky puppy pushed her down the little hole," she mused. "The mystery of Rose Hill is solved."

The little girls watched in awe as the tiny face was cleaned and the lovely hair was combed.

"She's surprisingly unhurt," commented Mrs. Jefferson.

"It's because she's so well made," replied Aunt Marge.

Jimbo, who had missed the fun of finding her, was allowed to choose which dress she would wear first. After Aunt Marge removed the soiled, blue-checked morning dress, Jimbo decided that she should be dressed in her blue velvet evening gown with the cape and the fur muff.

Mamselle was just dressed when Mr. Jefferson came home. All the shouts and exclamations were repeated for his benefit.

"Well," he suggested when he finally got the details of the day somewhat clarified, "even though there is no rose bloom to enter in the exhibit tomorrow, why don't you put Mamselle in the antique section as 'Plantation Doll'?"

CHAPTER TWENTY-TWO

THE BLUE RIBBON

Molly and Lucinda were dressed like a pair of little ladies in their yellow pinafores and their big straw hats. They wore black patent leather slippers and white socks, and they each had a pair of white gloves. They wanted to be dressed as nearly as possible like Mamselle.

They were going to the Flower and Antique Show. Lucinda held the small leather trunk of clothes, and Molly held Mamselle proudly on her lap. They had drawn straws to

make the decision as to who would carry the doll.

They were off early, as they wanted to get Mamselle entered before the show officially opened. Mrs. Jefferson had telephoned ahead to make sure that it wasn't too late for a last-minute entry. Aunt Marge had a little card with the information about Mamselle written on it.

The two mothers and the two little girls slipped into a side door at the Parish House where the committee was busy getting the last of the exhibits set up.

At last they got Mamselle in place, the lovely Plantation Doll dressed in her yellow afternoon dress with her tiny straw hat and her mitts and parasol.

Molly and Lucinda hardly left their spot near the doll all day. They loved hearing it over and over—people's excited exclamations over the beauty of the doll and the dramatic

way in which she had been found after all the years of being lost.

And of course they were there when the judges came by, making notes and whispering comments.

"I hope she'll win something," breathed Molly.

The girls closed their eyes when the committee came to place the ribbons. An excited burst of applause and congratulations made them open their eyes.

"Molly," cried Lucinda, "look! It's a blue ribbon!"

"Not *a* blue ribbon—*the* blue ribbon," breathed Molly as she looked more closely.

For there, pinned to the hem of Mamselle's tiny skirt, was a large gold-embossed ribbon which read:

Best Exhibit
Annual Antique Show